The Adventures of Tom Sawyer

Treasury of Illustrated Classics™

The Adventures of Tom Sawyer

by
Mark Twain

Adapted by
Tracy Christopher

Illustrated by
Ned Butterfield

Modern Publishing
A Division of Unisystems, Inc.
New York, New York 10022

Series UPC: 39340

Cover art by Ned Butterfield

Contents

Chapter

1

Aunt Polly's Fence

"Tom!"

No answer from Tom.

"Tom!"

Still no answer.

"Where is that boy, I wonder? Tom!"

Aunt Polly looked in the living room, then under the bed. She was about to yell out the back door when she heard a noise behind her. She grabbed Tom just in time. He had been in the pantry sneaking jam again. "I must have told you forty times to stay out of that jam, Tom Sawyer," she scolded.

She was about to spank him, too, when he said, "Look out behind you,

Aunt!" Aunt Polly let go and spun around. Her nephew ran out the door, climbed over the back fence, and disappeared.

Tom's Aunt Polly couldn't help but laugh. That rascal had tricked her again. He knew that if he made her laugh, she couldn't be angry at him. Still, Tom was too wild. She surely had her hands full with that nephew of hers.

At dinner that night, Aunt Polly discovered from Tom's damp collar that he

had skipped school to go swimming. But, once again, Tom ran outside before she could punish him.

It was a fine summer evening, and it wasn't dark yet. Tom had just learned how to whistle. He was walking down the street, practicing, when he saw a new boy on the corner. They were the same age, but the new boy had nicer clothes than Tom did. And he was wearing shoes!

This was Alfred Temple. He and Tom began making fun of each other. They walked in circles, pushing each other, daring each other to fight. Finally, they did fight. Tom chased the other boy home and stood outside his house. The two boys were still making faces at each other when the new boy's mother made Tom go home. She called him a mean, bad child.

When Tom got home, it was late and Aunt Polly was very angry. She took one look at Tom's torn clothes and figured that he had been fighting again. She would just have to punish him this time. She would make him work on Saturday, while all the other children were playing.

On Saturday morning, Tom stepped out of the house. He was carrying a bucket of whitewash and a paintbrush with a long handle. It was a beautiful day. Flowers were blooming, and the air was cool and sweet.

Tom sat down on a box and looked at the fence. Ninety feet of fence, six feet high! And he had to paint every inch of it! Tom sighed. He dipped his brush in the whitewash and ran it along the top board. Then he sat down again and looked sadly at the tiny patch he had painted.

Soon, the other boys would come out to play. They would have a great time making fun of him because he had to work on Saturday.

Tom took everything he had out of his pockets. Pieces of broken toys, marbles, trash—not enough to exchange with any of the boys to get them to work in his place.

Nothing worth even half an hour of freedom. Tom gave up the idea of trying to buy some help.

Then he had a brilliant idea. He picked up his brush and began to paint quite happily. Soon, Ben Rogers came along. He was eating an apple. That apple made Tom hungry!

Ben began to tease Tom. "Hello,

Tom," he said. "I'm going swimming. Don't you wish you could come, too? But you have to work, don't you?"

Tom said, "What do you call work? A boy doesn't get a chance to paint a fence every day, does he?" And Tom kept right on painting. He seemed to be having a lot of fun.

Ben got very interested. Soon, he said, "Hey, Tom. Let me paint a little. Please?"

Tom thought a minute. Then he said, "Well, Ben, Aunt Polly cares a lot about this fence. It has got to be done right. Very few boys could do this job the way she wants it done."

Ben begged Tom to let him try. He promised to be careful. When he offered Tom his apple, Tom finally let him have the brush. As Ben went to work, sweating in the sun, Tom sat on his box in the shade. He ate Ben's apple, and he made plans to trick more boys the way he had just tricked Ben.

By the end of the afternoon, Aunt

Polly's fence had three coats of whitewash on it. Tom was a lot richer than before. When Ben had become tired, Billy Fisher gave Tom a kite for a chance to paint. Other boys provided marbles, some chalk, a tin soldier, some tadpoles, some fire-crackers, a dog collar—but no dog—and a lot of other things. Tom had spent a great afternoon with plenty of company.

Tom went inside the house. He asked Aunt Polly if he could play, since the fence was finished. Aunt Polly couldn't believe Tom was telling the truth. Then she saw the entire fence, whitewashed three times! Even the ground around the fence was painted!

Aunt Polly said, "Well, Tom Sawyer. You do work when you want to. But you sure don't want to very often. All right, go on and play." And she gave Tom another apple as a reward!

Aunt Polly told Tom how good it always felt to be rewarded for hard work and good manners. Tom took a doughnut when she wasn't looking. He ran down the alley and went to find his friend, Joe Harper. Every Saturday, Tom and Joe played army. They were the two enemy generals. They gave the orders. Smaller kids were the soldiers who did the fighting. That afternoon, Tom's army won. The boys made another date to fight the next Saturday. Then everyone went home.

Chapter

②

Tom Falls in Love

Tom passed in front of Jeff Thatcher's house on his way home. There was a girl in the yard. Tom had never seen her before. She had blue eyes, and long blond hair tied in braids down her back.

Tom fell in love at first sight. He completely forgot about his other girlfriend, Amy Lawrence. Amy had agreed to be his girlfriend just the week before. Tom had been the happiest boy alive for seven days afterwards.

Now Tom began to show off for this new girl. She pretended not to notice him.

In fact, when he was doing one of his most dangerous tricks, she looked like she was going to go inside! But she threw a flower over the gate before she went in.

Tom picked up a stick. He began to balance it on his nose. He moved closer and closer to the flower on the ground. Finally, he picked it up with his toes and hopped down the street until he was out of sight. When no one was looking, he grabbed it off the ground and put it inside his shirt, close to his heart.

The next day was Sunday. Time for church. Tom had to learn some Bible verses before Sunday school. His cousin Mary had promised him a present if he could learn all five verses. He finally got them right, so Mary gave him a Barlow knife. It wouldn't cut anything, but it was brand-new. Tom was delighted.

Then it was time to wash. Mary gave Tom a big bowl of water and some soap to take outside. Tom carefully rolled up his sleeves. He dipped the bar of soap in the water to get it wet. Then he gently poured out all the water on the ground, without letting it touch his skin. He went back inside and pretended to dry his face on the towel by the door.

"You don't fool me, Tom Sawyer," Mary said, laughing. "Look at this dirty towel!" She gave him some more water. This time, Tom tried to wash. When he came back inside, he still had dirt on his neck! Mary helped him wash and comb his hair.

Tom had to put on his good clothes and his shoes. "Mary, do I have to wear shoes? They hurt my feet!" Tom yelled, kicking his shoes. He hated shoes more than anything. Mary managed to convince him to put them on. Then, Tom, Mary, and Sid, Tom's younger cousin, walked to Sunday school.

Tom stopped outside the door of the church. He asked his friend Bill if he would trade his yellow ticket for a piece of candy and a fish hook. Bill agreed to the trade. Tom traded some marbles and some small toys for red and blue tickets owned by other boys.

These tickets were rewards given by the Sunday school to children who could recite Bible verses by heart. A blue ticket was given if you could recite two verses. Ten blue tickets could be exchanged for one red ticket. Ten red tickets were worth one yellow ticket.

When you had ten yellow tickets, the Sunday school director gave you a Bible! That meant you had memorized two thousand verses. What a lot of work! Mary had won two Bibles, but it had taken two years. Only the older students were serious enough to learn their verses. But every student wanted to win a Bible. People thought you were so special on the day it was given to you!

Mr. Walters, the Sunday school director, began the morning with a long speech. It always lasted forever. The children were getting restless; then they saw visitors walking into the room.

There was an older man with gray hair, and a woman who was probably his wife. The visitors seemed very important. It was the great Judge Thatcher and his wife. They lived in a much bigger town, twelve whole miles away!

Judge Thatcher was holding his daughter's hand. It was the girl Tom had seen on Saturday—the one who had thrown the flower over the gate! She must be Jeff Thatcher's cousin.

Tom began to show off. He pushed the other boys, made faces, and pulled hair. He did everything he could to try to get her attention. Jeff Thatcher went up to shake hands with his uncle, the judge. All the boys wished they were Jeff, especially Tom. Then, Tom had a great idea for getting close to Judge Thatcher and the new girl.

All of a sudden, Tom Sawyer came forward and presented his tickets. He had nine yellow tickets, nine red tickets, and ten blue ones. Enough for a Bible!

Mr. Walters was very, very surprised. He thought Tom would never, ever have enough tickets for a Bible. Two thousand verses! He was more than a little suspicious, but he really wanted to impress Judge Thatcher. So, Tom was given a Bible.

"You're a fine young man, Thomas Sawyer," Judge Thatcher declared. "You understand that learning is worth more than gold. Knowledge makes great men, and good men."

"Yes, sir!" Tom agreed happily as the blond girl smiled at him.

"Well, Tom, why don't you tell us some of the things you have learned in this fine Sunday school. Let's start with a simple question. Can you tell me the names of two of the apostles?"

Tom didn't know, of course, but he couldn't tell that to the judge. So he took a guess, and gave his answer loudly and with great conviction. "David and Goliath, sir!" That certainly wasn't the right answer. Luckily for Tom, it was time for the church service to begin.

Children sat with their parents for the church service. Aunt Polly always made Tom sit far away from the window, hoping he might pay attention to the service. Tom always found other things to do, though. Right after the opening prayer, he caught a fly in his hands, but Aunt Polly made him let it go.

Tom waited until his aunt was absorbed in the sermon, then he got out his pinch-bug, which he kept in a small box. It was a black beetle with big jaws that could pinch things. Tom tried to pick it up, but it pinched his finger. When he finally shook it off, it landed in the middle of the aisle, out of Tom's reach. But it had landed on its back, so it couldn't crawl away.

No one seemed to notice the bug at first, but then a poodle belonging to one of the people at church walked by. He found the pinch-bug and played with it. He got too close, though, and the bug pinched his nose! The dog yelped and quickly shook it off, and the pinch-bug landed on

its back again. People nearby began to smile, but they couldn't let themselves laugh out loud during the sermon!

The poodle came over again. When he got tired of teasing the bug, he followed an ant around. But then he forgot all about the pinch-bug and accidentally sat down on it! This time, the pinch-bug pinched him on the rear and didn't let go. The dog began to run all around the church until he finally ran out the door. By that time, a lot of people were laughing out loud. Soon, the service was over. Everyone was relieved, except Tom. That poodle had run away with his pinch-bug!

Chapter

③

The Sore Toe

On Monday morning Tom was miserable because he knew he had to go to school. He wished he were sick. Then maybe he wouldn't have to go. Tom didn't feel sick, but maybe his stomach hurt. No, his stomach didn't hurt one bit. He did have that tooth he had knocked loose, but he didn't want Aunt Polly to pull it out. He would save the loose tooth for later.

Then Tom remembered hearing the doctor talking about something that could make you sick for almost two or three weeks. You could even lose a finger!

But Tom couldn't remember any of the other symptoms.

Tom looked at his sore toe. Maybe you could lose a toe instead of a finger. Maybe the sore toe would be enough to convince Aunt Polly he should stay home from school. He began to make a lot of groaning noises. Finally, Tom's cousin, Sid, woke up. Tom groaned some more. He sounded really sick. Sid ran downstairs to find Aunt Polly.

"Oh, Aunt Polly! Come quick! Tom's dying!" Sid cried.

"Dying! That's nonsense! I don't believe it," Aunt Polly said. But she ran upstairs, anyway.

Tom had such a good imagination that, by this time, he really thought he was sick.

"Tom, what is the matter? What on earth is the matter with you?" Aunt Polly asked. She was very worried.

"Oh, Auntie, my sore toe is going to fall off!" Tom groaned.

Aunt Polly sat down. She laughed a little. Then she cried a little. She said, "Tom, you really scared me for a minute. Now, you just stop this. Be quiet and get out of that bed!"

The pain disappeared, and Tom felt a little foolish. "But it hurt so much, I couldn't even feel my loose tooth."

"Which tooth? Open your mouth. Well, it is loose, but you are certainly not going to die from it. Mary, get me some thread and a coal from the fire," Aunt Polly said.

"Oh, Auntie, please don't pull it out," Tom begged. "It doesn't hurt anymore. I really don't want to stay home from school."

"So that's it! All this fuss because you thought you would get to stay home and go fishing instead. Tom Sawyer, I love you so much. Even when you try to break my heart with your tricks!"

So, Tom got his tooth pulled and got sent to school. On his way, he saw Huckleberry Finn and stopped to talk to him. Huck's father didn't take very good care of him. Huck never went to school or to church. He wore his father's old clothes, which were way too big for him.

Aunt Polly had forbidden Tom to play with Huck. Like all the other parents, she thought that Huck was a bad influence on any good boy. But all the good boys wanted to be like Huck—Tom included. Huck could go fishing or swimming whenever he wanted to. He could stay up late. He never had to wash. And

he didn't have to obey anybody. Tom and all the other boys played with Huck every chance they got.

Huck was carrying a dead cat. He said that they were good to take off warts, those little bumps on your skin. You had to take the cat to the graveyard at night. At midnight a devil would come, or maybe two or three. You couldn't see them, but you'd hear a noise like the wind. Sometimes you could even hear the devils talking! Then, when the devils were taking away a dead body, you'd throw the dead cat at them. You'd have to say, "Devil follow body. Cat follow devil. Warts follow cat. I'm done with you!" Pretty soon after that, the warts would just disappear.

Tom wanted to go with Huck to the graveyard. The devils would surely come for Hoss Williams's dead body that night. Huck said he would come to Tom's house after dark and meow like a cat under Tom's window. Then they would walk to the graveyard together.

Tom was about to say good-bye to Huck when he noticed that Huck was carrying a small bug. It was a tick, one of the first ticks of the season. Tom offered to trade his tooth for it. Huck agreed. Tom put the tick in the box he had used for his pinch-bug. Then the boys said good-bye, each feeling richer than before.

Tom hurried into school. The teacher asked him why he was so late. Tom was about to tell a lie when he noticed that the new Thatcher girl was watching him. He also saw that there was a seat next to her on the girls' side of the room.

Tom knew that the teacher would probably punish him by making him sit with the girls. So, Tom decided to tell the truth. "I stopped to talk to Huckleberry Finn," he said.

This was worse than a lie, because the teacher thought Huck was a bad boy, just like all the other adults did. Tom was sent to sit with the girls. But he was secretly quite content, even when the other boys made fun of him.

The new girl made faces at Tom. Then she turned away and wouldn't look at him. When she turned back around, Tom had put a peach on her desk. She pushed it away. Tom put it back. She pushed it away again, but she seemed less angry. Tom put it back. This time, she let it stay there.

Tom wrote on his little chalkboard, "Please take it. I have more." The girl glanced at the words, but she didn't say

anything. Tom began to draw something. He worked for a long time, pretending to ignore the girl. She got very curious.

Soon, she asked to see the drawing. Tom showed her a house with two chimneys. "Draw a man," she whispered, and Tom complied. "Now draw me walking up to the house." Tom drew an hourglass with long blond hair. "I wish I could draw like that," she said softly.

"I'll teach you at lunchtime, if you want." She nodded yes. "What's your name?" Tom finally dared to ask.

"Becky Thatcher. What's yours?"

"Thomas Sawyer. But that's what they call me when they're mad at me. You'll call me Tom, won't you?"

Tom began to write again on his slate. This time, he wouldn't let Becky see. Finally she grabbed the slate away from him. He had written "I love you" on it. Becky said, "Oh, you bad thing." She slapped Tom's hand. She turned red, too. She looked happy, though.

Just then, the teacher came over. He made Tom move back to his seat on the boys' side. The whole class giggled, but Tom didn't care. For the rest of the morning, Tom tried to study. He couldn't concentrate. He made so many mistakes in spelling that he lost the spelling contest. He had to give up the medal he had worn for months. Another student would get to show off now.

Chapter

④

Tom's Engagement

The morning dragged on. Would the noon recess ever come? It was hot and sunny outside. Cardiff Hill looked green and shady in the distance. The students in Tom's class were very quiet. Most of them were reading or writing. Some of them were trying not to fall asleep.

Luckily, it was time for lunch. Tom and Becky just pretended to go home. They sat down at Becky's desk, and Tom showed Becky how to draw a house and other things.

When Becky was tired of drawing, they began to talk. Tom told her all about the circus. Becky said that her father had promised to take her there for her birthday. Tom said he wanted to be a clown when he grew up. Becky thought that would be nice.

Then, Tom said, "Becky, have you ever been engaged to be married? Would you like to?"

"Maybe," she said. "I don't know. What is it like?"

"It's not like anything," Tom explained. "You just tell a boy that you won't be with anybody but him, never ever. Then you kiss, and that's all."

"Kiss? Why do you kiss?" Becky wondered.

"They always do that."

"Everybody?"

"Why yes, they do it because they're in love, I guess. Do you remember what I wrote on the slate?"

"Yes, but I won't tell you," Becky said shyly.

"Let me tell you again," Tom said. "I'll whisper it."

So Tom whispered in Becky's ear that he loved her. Becky said it, too. Then Tom kissed her. He said, "Now you can't ever love anybody but me, forever. Will you?"

"No, I'll never love anybody but you, Tom," Becky promised. "I'll never marry anybody but you. You can't marry anybody but me, either."

"Of course not. That's part of it. And we will always walk to school together, when nobody's looking. And you choose me and I'll choose you at parties. That's what you do when you're engaged," Tom explained.

"It's so nice. I've never heard of it before."

"Oh, it's great to be engaged. Amy Lawrence and I . . ."

Becky's big eyes told Tom that he had said something he shouldn't have.

"Oh, Tom!" Becky cried. "You've been engaged before!"

Becky began to cry. Tom tried to fix things, but Becky wouldn't stop crying. He said that he didn't love Amy Lawrence anymore, but Becky wouldn't talk to him. Tom even tried to give Becky the best thing he owned—a brass doorknob. But when he put it in front of her, she just threw it on the floor.

That made Tom so mad, he ran away from Becky. He didn't go back to school that afternoon. Tom ran off to Cardiff Hill. He crossed the creek several times so that no one could follow his tracks. Then he went into the woods behind the Widow Douglas's house. Tom found his special spot in the woods and sat down under a tree to think.

Tom was so unhappy, he wished he were dead. Why was Becky so angry with him? How could she treat him this way? She would sure feel horrible if she found out he really was dead. But her tears

would be too late. There was some satis-
faction in that. Oh, why couldn't a person die for just a little while!

Tom sighed in frustration. What if he
left St. Petersburg and never came back?
Becky would sure miss him then. He

would run away and become a clown in the circus. No, that was silly. He would be a soldier and come back home after a long time, a hero.

No, he would become an Indian. That was even better. He would hunt buffalo and come back a big chief. He would ride into Sunday school on his horse, wearing feathers and war paint. Everyone would be jealous of him.

Tom thought some more until he had an even better idea. He would be a pirate. That was it! He would search for treasure on the high seas. People would be afraid of him. He would come back to St. Petersburg in his fancy pirate clothes. People would see his black flag with the skull on it, and they would say, "It's Tom Sawyer, the Pirate! The Black Avenger!"

It was settled. Tom would leave the next day. But first, he had to get everything out of his hiding place. Tom took out the Barlow knife Mary had given him and began to dig with it. Soon, he hit wood that sounded hollow. He reached in the hole and said, "What hasn't come here, come! What is here, stay here!"

Tom pulled a wooden box from the hole. He looked inside. There was only the same blue marble he had put in there two weeks ago. Where were all the other marbles? When you buried a marble and said the right spell, all the marbles you had ever lost were supposed to come back to the one you'd hidden. But it hadn't worked for Tom. He told himself that a witch must have broken his spell.

Suddenly, Tom heard a tin horn blowing in the woods. It was Joe Harper. Joe was dressed to play Robin Hood. Tom's sword and trumpet were hidden in the leaves behind a log. He grabbed them and went to have a sword fight with Joe.

Tom and Joe were good with swords—two hits up, two hits down. Tom played Robin Hood, so he was supposed to win. It said so in the book. Joe had to pretend to fall down and die.

Joe wanted Tom to take a turn dying, too. They changed places. Tom shot his last arrow and said, "Where this arrow falls, bury me there under the greenwood tree." Then he fell back and pretended to die.

The two boys were very happy after their game of Robin Hood. They decided they would rather live in Sherwood Forest for a year than be president of the United States forever.

Chapter

(5)

Murder at the Graveyard

That Monday night, Tom and Sid were sent to bed at nine-thirty. Sid was soon fast asleep, but Tom stayed awake and listened for Huck's meow. As he lay in bed, he heard lots of night noises. The clock was ticking. A dog was howling. The wind in the trees outside. Then he heard the clock strike. It was only ten o'clock! It felt as if he had been waiting forever. He didn't want to, but he was falling asleep.

At eleven o'clock, someone threw a bottle out the window next door because a cat was meowing like crazy! It was really Huck, of course. Tom became wide awake when he heard the bottle hit the shed. He got dressed in an instant. Then he climbed out the window very quietly.

Huck was waiting for Tom by the tool-shed. He had the dead cat with him. The boys walked in the moonlight to the grave-yard. It was the old Western kind, full of

sunken graves and old, wooden markers lying at crazy angles all around. Most of the paint had come off the wood, so you couldn't tell anymore who was buried where. Tall grasses grew everywhere, and enormous trees tangled the oldest graves in their roots.

Huck and Tom decided to hide near the newest grave, where Hoss Williams was buried. Three large elm trees grew nearby. The two boys would be protected by the three trunks, which grew together to make a sort of wall. They sat down and waited for the devils to come.

At first, everything was quiet. An owl hooted. Then the boys heard a different noise. It sounded like voices! A light was coming up the hill. The devils were coming for Hoss Williams!

The boys were really scared. They stayed hidden and were absolutely still. As the voices came closer, Huck recognized three men, not devils at all! It was Injun Joe, his friend Muff Potter, and another man, Doctor Robinson. What were they doing in the graveyard at midnight?

The boys didn't move a muscle and didn't speak a word. The men couldn't see them. Doc Robinson put the lantern next to the new grave. Then he sat down

by one of the trees. He was so close, Tom could have touched him!

Injun Joe and Muff Potter got two shovels from the wheelbarrow they had brought and began to dig. They were going to dig up Hoss Williams's coffin.

This was against the law. Both boys knew that. It was also against the law to study dead bodies. That was probably what Doc Robinson wanted to do. He had probably paid the two men to steal this body from the grave.

The shovels hit the wooden coffin with a thump. Injun Joe dumped the body out of the coffin and put it in the wheelbarrow. Muff Potter put a blanket over the body and tied it down with some rope.

Muff Potter cut the end of the rope with his knife. Then he said, "We want more money. Or we won't move this body anywhere."

"I've already paid you," Doctor Robinson said.

"You've done more than that," Injun Joe hissed. He was very angry. "Maybe you don't remember the time your father said I was no good. He had me jailed. Well, I haven't forgotten. You'll pay more or else."

Injun Joe grabbed the doctor, but Doc Robinson hit him. Muff Potter tried to help his friend, but the doctor hit him, too, with a big piece of wood. Muff was knocked unconscious. Injun Joe picked up the knife Muff Potter had dropped. Doc didn't see the knife until it was too late. The doctor fell on top of Muff Potter, dead.

Huck and Tom were so frightened that they ran down the hill as fast and as quietly as they could. They kept on running until they reached a big warehouse on the other side of town. They hid in the back room and rested there.

When they could breathe again, Tom whispered, "What do you think will happen now, Huck?"

"Doc Robinson is dead. If they ever catch Injun Joe, they'll hang him for murder," Huck said.

"Do you really think so?"

"I know so!"

"Do you think we should tell what we saw?" Tom asked.

"Look here, Tom," said Huck. "What if Injun Joe finds out we told on him?

He'll kill us for telling! Let Muff Potter tell the whole story."

"But Muff Potter doesn't know what happened! He was out cold! He didn't see anything!" Tom reminded Huck.

"Well, if we tell, Injun Joe will kill us. That's certain. We have to swear not to ever tell. That's all there is to it."

Tom found a piece of wood. He wrote on it, "Huck Finn and Tom Sawyer swear

they won't tell. They'll drop down dead if they ever do, and rot." Both boys signed their names. They buried the piece of wood in the dirt floor.

Tom and Huck were about to leave when they heard a dog howl. It was a stray dog. When stray dogs howled, it meant that somebody would die soon. Everybody knew that. The dog was just standing there, howling. He seemed to be pointing at something in the shed behind the warehouse. Huck and Tom crept over to the shed and looked in the doorway. To their horror, they saw Muff Potter sound asleep in the shed. Muff was going to die soon!

The boys had seen enough for one night. They ran for home. When they got to Tom's house, they promised once more not to tell what they had seen at the graveyard. Then Tom climbed back in through his bedroom window.

Sid was snoring as Tom got into bed. But Sid was really awake. The next morning, he told Aunt Polly that Tom had been out almost all night. When Tom went down to breakfast, everyone was quiet. No one would look at him.

After breakfast, Aunt Polly took Tom to the kitchen. She began to cry as she told Tom that she had given up on him. He would probably never be a good boy. She was tired of trying to make him be good.

Tom felt awful. Aunt Polly was really upset. This was much worse than a spanking. Tom promised never to go out at night again. He promised to try harder to be a good boy. He said he was sorry. Eventually, Aunt Polly forgave him and sent him to school.

As soon as Tom got to school, he and Joe Harper got punished for having cut class the day before. To make matters worse, when Tom got back to his desk he found something wrapped in paper—it was his brass doorknob. Becky Thatcher had refused his gift! This was going to be a terrible day.

It was a terrible day, indeed. By noon, the whole town of St. Petersburg knew that Doc Robinson had been killed out at the graveyard. School was closed for that afternoon.

Tom went to the graveyard with all the other people of the town. He couldn't help himself. When he got there, he saw Huck Finn. The two boys looked at each other, but they didn't speak. They were afraid that someone might see them

talking, especially Injun Joe. He was there, too, standing around the grave just like everyone else. He looked so calm! The boys couldn't believe he was there.

Just then, somebody saw Muff Potter and the sheriff coming up the hill. Muff looked confused and scared. The sheriff was holding him by the arm.

When they got to the scene of the crime, the sheriff held up a knife. He asked, "Is this your knife, Muff Potter?"

Muff said yes, then he began to cry. He said, "You better tell the sheriff what happened, Injun Joe. I can't remember."

Injun Joe stood there and told a big lie. He said that Doc Robinson and Muff Potter had been fighting—and that Muff had stabbed the doctor! Tom and Huck couldn't believe it. Injun Joe was lying, but God didn't strike him down with lightning. He was lying, but the sheriff and even Muff Potter believed him. He even swore on the Bible that he was telling the truth.

The sheriff wrote down Injun Joe's story. The boys wanted to tell what had really happened. But they were too afraid. Maybe Injun Joe was a devil after all. Then he would kill them for sure.

Tom and Huck left the crowd and went home. Tom felt awful. Muff Potter was innocent. Yet even Muff Potter thought he had killed the doctor. Even he believed Injun Joe, along with everyone else in town.

Tom wanted to tell the truth, but he was scared. He had promised Huck he wouldn't tell. Huck would be in danger, too, if Injun Joe found out Tom had told.

For two weeks, Tom had bad dreams. Sid said Tom talked in his sleep, but he couldn't understand what he was saying. Aunt Polly made Tom take baths and drink lots of medicine that tasted bad. Nothing helped.

Chapter

6

Pirates on Jackson's Island

Poor Tom! He had had enough trouble. To make things worse, Becky Thatcher got sick. She didn't go to school for two weeks. Every day, Tom waited by the school yard gate, wishing he would see her walking down the road. Every day, when Tom saw Becky's cousin, Jeff, he listened to hear if Jeff would say something about Becky. Most nights, Tom spent some time outside her house, hoping to see her through the window. No one knew how much Tom worried about Becky, or how much he missed her, not even Jeff Thatcher.

Tom was full of joy the day Becky came back to school. He began to show off as soon as she came into the school yard. He ran all over. He did cartwheels and handsprings. He did everything he could think of to make Becky notice him. Finally, after all his efforts, all Becky said was, "Some people think they are so smart—always showing off!" And she walked away.

That just about did it! Tom was tired of everybody. No one loved him. He would run away. Then they would all be so sorry when they found out he was gone, especially Becky Thatcher.

Tom walked down the road. He was thinking what a poor, friendless boy he was when he ran into Joe Harper. Joe was as sad and as angry as Tom. Joe's mother had just punished him for drinking all the cream. But he hadn't even seen the cream! She was wrong, and it wasn't fair.

Tom said that he was planning to run away and be a pirate. Joe thought this was a great idea. He asked Tom if he could be a pirate, too. Tom agreed, and the two friends began to plan their new adventure.

Tom and Joe were still planning when they saw Huck Finn. Huck thought

it might be fun to be a pirate, too. He had nothing better to do. So, the three boys agreed to meet at the river after dark that night.

At midnight, Tom was on a high hill looking down at the Mississippi River. He whistled a signal. Soon, he heard some-one whistle back. Then, a voice said, "Who goes there?"

"Tom Sawyer, the Black Avenger," Tom answered. "Name your names."

"Huck Finn, the Red-handed."

"Joe Harper, the Terror of the Seas."

"Good," said Tom. "What's the secret password?"

"Blood!" the two other boys cried out in a loud whisper.

When Tom heard the password, he climbed down the hill. Joe and Huck were waiting on the path that ran along the river. Tom had brought a big ham and some corn bread he had taken from the kitchen. Joe had a lot of bacon, some fish hooks, and line. Huck had a frying pan.

Nobody had thought of matches to make a fire, so the boys crept onto a big boat and took a coal from the fire. They carried it in the frying pan.

The boys walked about two miles on the path, until they were far upstream from the town of St. Petersburg. They knew there was a raft there that hadn't been used in a long time. Tom loaded the raft, then Huck and Joe pushed it off the bank and hopped on. The pirates were headed down the Mississippi River!

Huck used the big paddle. Joe was in the back, guiding the raft. Tom stood in the middle and gave orders. He was the pirate captain, after all. The boys floated down the river for about two hours. They could see a few small lights in St. Petersburg as they passed by it. Everyone in town was asleep. The pirates realized they might never see their families or friends again.

Tom thought about his Aunt Polly. Joe thought about his mother. But the

excitement of being pirates overshadowed any misgivings Tom and Joe had about leaving their families. They were headed for Jackson's Island, a small island on the Mississippi. No one lived there, and no one from St. Petersburg ever went there, although it wasn't that far from town. No one would find them on Jackson's Island.

Their pirate island had woods and a spring with fresh water. It was the perfect place to bury all the treasure they would take as pirates. Soon, they would

have gold and silver, diamonds, and fancy clothes!

The raft hit the sand of Jackson's Island. The boys jumped out and unloaded. They used an old sail they'd found on the raft to make a tent for their things. They didn't need a tent for themselves. They would sleep outside, under the stars, like real pirates.

The boys made a fire against a giant log in the woods. They cooked some bacon in the frying pan and ate it with some of the corn bread Tom had brought. After dinner, the boys lay around the fire. Joe and Tom told Huck everything they had ever read or heard about pirates. They couldn't wait to begin! But they were all so sleepy.

Soon, the boys stopped talking. Huck fell to sleep right away. Joe and Tom had a harder time of it. Each boy felt guilty, although he'd never say it out loud. Their families would be worried sick about them. Also, they had both stolen things from their kitchens. Tom had taken a ham. Joe had carried off a whole side of bacon! This was different from taking small things like candy or apples. This was really stealing.

Tom said his prayers silently. He promised never to steal anything again. Joe did the same, although Tom didn't know it. These were strange promises, since pirates usually made their living stealing treasure. But at least Tom and Joe were finally able to fall asleep.

The next morning, Tom was the first boy awake. He lay there watching the light change from gray to white as the sun rose. Birds began to sing loudly. An ant came by carrying a dead spider five times bigger than it was. A green caterpillar crawled from a leaf onto Tom's leg. This made Tom very happy. When an inchworm "measured" your leg like that, it meant that you would get new clothes. Tom was hoping for a pirate costume.

Soon the other boys were up. They all ran to the shallow water near the sandbar

for a swim. Their raft had disappeared. It had drifted away down the river during the night. The boys told themselves it didn't matter. They didn't ever want to leave Jackson's Island, anyway.

When they were hungry, Joe made a fire. Tom and Huck went fishing. Their hooks had barely touched the water when

the fish began to bite. Soon they had caught enough river bass and catfish to feed an army of pirates. Joe fried the fish with some bacon. None of them had ever tasted anything so good!

After breakfast, the boys explored the island. Jackson's Island was about three miles long and a quarter of a mile wide. It was closer to one bank of the river than the other. At one point, it was so close that you could swim to the Illinois shore if you wanted to.

The boys spent most of the afternoon walking around the island, stopping to swim whenever it got too hot. When they returned to camp, they were too tired to fish, so they ate some cold ham and lay around awhile. It was quiet and peaceful, the perfect afternoon for a nap.

All of a sudden, Tom heard a big, booming noise, like thunder. But there was no sign of rain. Then the noise came again. Boom! The noise was coming from upriver, near St. Petersburg.

The boys walked to the tip of the island to take a look. Far upstream, they could see the town's ferryboat with a cannon mounted on deck. The cannon was making that loud booming noise. There were also about ten rowboats on the river, floating around the ferryboat. The boys couldn't see what the men in the boats were doing. Nobody could see the boys, either. The island was too far away. But the men seemed to be looking for something.

"I know," said Tom. "Somebody drowned!"

"Yes, that's it," Huck agreed. "They did that last summer when Bill Turner drowned. They shoot a cannon over the water. It makes the body come up to the top of the water."

"I sure wish I was over there now," Joe said eagerly.

"Me, too," said Huck. "I wish I knew who it was who drowned."

The boys listened and watched. Suddenly, Tom realized who it was the

men were looking for. "Boys, I know who drowned. It's us!" he cried happily.

This was very exciting. The boys felt like heroes. People back home thought they were dead! Their families were probably really sad and sorry about all the times they had punished them. They were probably wishing that Tom and Joe and Huck would give them just one more chance, because they would never be mean or unfair again. Oh, how people must miss those poor boys!

Chapter

7

Sneaking Back to Town

The happy pirates watched the search parties on the river until the sun went down. When they went back to camp, they fried some more fish for dinner.

Having full stomachs made the boys sleepy. They lay around the fire and summed up their first day on the island.

"Those fish tasted almost as good as the ones we had for breakfast," Tom said contentedly.

"Tomorrow, after we go fishing, we can watch the town search for us some more." Huck was very excited that people cared enough to drag the river for him. "I bet all the boys in St. Petersburg wish they could be pirates like us. And now the whole town's talking about us 'cause we're dead. This is the life!"

Joe listened to Huck without saying anything. He was thinking about how sad his mother must be, and he suddenly felt very homesick. He felt guilty for making everyone worry about him. "It's not right, Huck, worrying everybody this way. Can't we go back for just a few days, to let them know we're all right?"

Tom was thinking the same thing, but he wouldn't admit it. "We just got here, Joe. We haven't even had a chance to look for buried treasure yet!"

Joe didn't want his friends to think he was a homesick baby, so he quickly agreed to stay on the island a few more days.

It was late when Huck and Joe finally fell asleep. Tom was still awake, though, and he was restless. Maybe Joe was right. Maybe he should sneak back to town for just one night. He would check on things and then come back to the island.

Tom left his place by the fire without waking the others. He found two big pieces of bark from a sycamore tree. The bark was smooth, almost like paper. Tom wrote a message for Joe on one piece, and put it in Joe's hat. Joe would find it when he woke up the next morning.

Tom also put some gifts for Joe and Huck in the hat. He gave up his best

toys—a big piece of chalk, a rubber ball, three fish hooks, and a marble that was made of real crystal. These things were really valuable. Tom hoped that Joe and Huck would understand what he was about to do.

Tom wrote another message on a second piece of bark. This one would be for his Aunt Polly. He would leave it somewhere in town for her to find. Tom put this piece of bark in his pocket. Then he quickly left his sleeping friends behind. He walked quickly through the woods to the place where Jackson's Island was close to the Illinois shore. He waded into the river until the water reached his waist, then he swam the rest of the way to shore.

Tom found a low spot on the bank. He pulled himself out of the river. His clothes were dripping wet, but the piece of bark was still nice and dry. He walked two miles upriver, until he saw the ferryboat. It was ten o'clock. He was just in time. The ferry was about to make its last trip of the day across the river to St. Petersburg.

Tom couldn't get on the ferry with the other passengers, of course, since he was still a pirate and a dead boy to boot. But there was a rowboat tied to the back of the ferry. Tom crawled into it and lay down under the seat. No one could see him from the ferry or from the shore.

Tom traveled across the river to the Missouri shore and slipped quietly into the water. He drifted downriver until no one could see him climb out onto shore. Then he ran through the empty back alleys of the town until he reached his own house. There was a light in the living room, where Aunt Polly usually slept. Tom peeked in the window. Sid, Mary, and Aunt Polly were sitting with Mrs. Harper, Joe's mother. They were talking, and they all looked very sad, except for Sid, maybe.

Tom crept around to the door and opened it just a little. He got down on his hands and knees. No one would see him if he crawled inside. He could hide under Aunt Polly's bed. He opened the door a little wider so he could squeeze through. The night breeze coming in made the candle flutter.

"Why is the candle blowing like that?" Aunt Polly wondered. "The door must have blown open. Go shut it, Sid." Tom was already inside and under the bed when Sid shut the door. That was a close one!

Tom lay on the floor under the bed in the living room. He could almost touch Aunt Polly's foot, and he could hear everything everyone was saying. They were talking about the missing boys, of course.

"Tom wasn't really bad," Aunt Polly said. "He was just playful and wild. He had no more sense than a puppy. And he was just as irresponsible. But he never meant to do anything bad. He was so generous and smart!"

Aunt Polly began to cry. So did Mrs. Harper. "My Joe was just the same," she said. "Always playing tricks, but just as nice as he could be. When I think that I spanked my poor Joe. He never did drink that cream. I threw it out myself because it was sour. But I forgot I did it and blamed him. Now I'll never see my poor boy again!" Joe's mother cried like her heart was breaking.

"I hope Tom is happy where he is," said Sid. "I hope he's in heaven. If only he hadn't been such a bad boy."

"Sid!" Aunt Polly glared at Tom's

cousin. "Don't you say anything bad about my Tom. God will take care of Tom Sawyer. There is no doubt about that, young man."

Listening to all this brought tears to Tom's eyes. Mary was saying nice things about him, too. Tom began to see how sweet and lovable he was. His family sure did miss him!

Tom wanted to run over to Aunt Polly and give her a big hug. He was very curious, though, so he just lay still and kept listening. Mrs. Harper was talking about how the town was searching for Tom and the other lost boys.

Mrs. Harper talked about how people had discovered the boys were gone that morning. Someone had noticed that the old raft was missing, too. Everyone concluded that the boys had taken the raft downriver to the next town. They thought the boys would surely come back when they were hungry. But that afternoon, someone found the empty raft five or six miles downriver. That was a bad sign. The

boys were all good swimmers, but the Mississippi was a big, deep river. Maybe they had drowned!

By late afternoon, people were so worried that they'd sent out the ferryboat and the rowboats. But no one found anything. Almost twenty-four hours had passed since the boys were last seen. It was now Wednesday night. If the boys were not found by Saturday, their families would have to give up. The town would hold a funeral service in the church on Sunday.

Mrs. Harper became so sad then that she had to leave Aunt Polly and go home. Aunt Polly sent Sid and Mary to bed. She got down on her knees by her own bed and said a long prayer for Tom. She said such nice things about him that Tom began to cry softly. Aunt Polly loved him very, very much. He could see that, now.

Finally, Aunt Polly fell asleep, and Tom crept out from under the bed. He watched her sleeping for a while. He took out the sycamore scroll from his pocket and silently read his message: "We are not dead. We are only off being pirates."

Tom was about to leave his message on the table near Aunt Polly's bed when

he had another brilliant idea. Wouldn't it be exciting if the pirates went to their own funeral on Sunday? That would be the best adventure ever!

Tom put the note for Aunt Polly back in his pocket. He kissed his aunt softly as she lay sleeping, and slipped quietly out of the house.

Chapter

8

Tom's Secret

Tom went back to the ferryboat. There was no one onboard except the night watchman, who was fast asleep. Tom untied the rowboat from the back of the ferry. People would think it had come untied and floated down the river by itself. Tom rowed across to the Illinois shore.

Rowing was hard work. It was getting very late, and Tom was tired and sleepy. He had to rest before going on. When he felt better, he walked two miles down the shore, but he had to stop and rest again when he reached the spot across from Jackson's Island.

The sun was coming up when Tom swam across to the island. He had to rest one more time before walking back to camp. It was hot and sunny by the time he finally arrived. Tom stopped at the edge of the woods when he heard his friends talking about him in camp. Joe

was saying to Huck, "Tom will come back, Huck, I'm sure he will. He must be planning something. I wonder what?"

Huck was looking hopefully at all the treasure Tom had left in Joe's hat. "These things Tom left belong to us now, don't they?"

"Almost, but not quite yet," Joe explained. "The message says they will belong to us if Tom isn't back here in time for breakfast."

"I am here for breakfast!" Tom cried. He stepped into camp. "I'm hungry, too!"

During breakfast, Tom told Joe and Huck how he had gone back to St. Petersburg that night. He was careful not to tell all the sad parts of the story, because Joe might get too homesick. He didn't tell them about the funeral on Sunday, either. He wanted to save that news for later. That was his secret, for the time being.

After breakfast, Tom decided to take a long nap in the shade. He had been awake all night. Joe and Huck spent the morning fishing and exploring the island.

Tom felt much better after his nap, so the whole gang went hunting for turtle eggs in the afternoon. The boys walked along the beach carrying long sticks. They poked them in the sand, looking for soft places. If they discovered one, they would dig very carefully, hoping to find eggs under the sand. Turtle eggs were small, about the size of a walnut shell, and white. Sometimes there were as many as sixty eggs in one hole.

The boys took only some of the eggs. They put the sand back over the rest and left them alone. That night and the next morning, they had scrambled turtle eggs with their bacon!

Friday was another hot and sunny day. The pirates spent all morning playing in the river. They swam and dove and wrestled in the water. They splashed each other, getting closer and closer, until one boy would try to dunk his neighbor.

When the boys were tired of swimming, they lay on the hot sand for a while. Tom decided that their pink skin made them look like clowns, so he drew a big circle in the sand and they all did clown tricks in the ring. They did cartwheels, handsprings, and somersaults. They even made human pyramids. When that got boring, they all got out their marbles. They played "knuck" and "keeps" and "ringtaw" until they didn't want to play anymore.

Huck and Joe decided to go swimming again. But Tom had lost the string of rattlesnake rattles that he wore around his ankle. Snake rattles protected you against stomach cramps when you were swimming. Everybody knew that. Tom was sure he would drown if he didn't have his lucky charm. He stayed on the beach, watching his friends swim.

When Huck and Joe came back, they flopped down in the shade beside Tom. The pirates were very, very tired. Too tired to play. Too tired to talk. Each boy was quiet, thinking. Tom wrote the name "Becky" in the sand with his toe. He got mad at himself for thinking of her, and erased her name. Then he wrote it again. He couldn't help it.

Joe Harper was looking toward St. Petersburg, barely visible upriver. Joe was thinking about his mother, and about how much he missed her. He was feeling more and more homesick.

Huck looked pretty sad, too. Tom

tried to cheer everyone up. "Let's go hunt
for buried treasure. I'm sure other pirates
must have left some here on the island!"

Joe didn't want to hunt for treasure.
He was poking at the ground with a
stick. Suddenly, he said, "Look, Tom. I
really want to go home."

"Don't you want to go fishing?"
Tom asked.

"I'm tired of fishing. I'm lonely, too."

"But we'll never find a spot for
swimming as nice as this one," Tom
pointed out.

"It's not as much fun when your mom's not there to tell you you can't go in the water," Joe sniffed.

"The baby's homesick," Tom teased. "The baby wants to go home to Momma."

"I miss my mom. So what? You would, too, if you had one," Joe said. He was angry because Tom was bothering him.

"Well, you just go on home, then. We don't need you, anyway. Huck and I will stay here by ourselves, won't we, Huck?"

"I guess so," Huck said. But he didn't sound too thrilled at the idea.

"Well, that's just fine with me," Joe declared. "I'll never speak to you again as long as I live, Tom Sawyer."

Joe got dressed and waded out into the river. He didn't even say good-bye. Huck watched Joe move toward the shore. He really wanted to go with him. He was ready to leave the island, too.

"Tom," Huck said, "it's going to be even more lonely without Joe. Let's go with him. Please?"

"I'm not leaving," Tom said. He was stubborn. "You just go on without me. I'm not stopping you."

"Are you sure you won't come with us, Tom?" Huck begged. "We'll wait on the shore for you."

"You and Joe will be waiting there a long, long, time," Tom declared. He was as stubborn as a mule.

Huck put on his clothes and waded out after Joe. Tom watched them leave. It

got so quiet and lonely all of a sudden! Tom wasn't sure he could stay on the island by himself after all, without his friends.

"Wait, wait!" Tom finally shouted. "I've got a secret I want to tell you."

Joe and Huck stopped in their tracks and turned around. Curiosity got the best of them and they headed back to the island. Tom told them about his secret plan. He was willing to leave the island soon. But couldn't they all wait until Sunday? They could hide in the church and listen to their own funeral service! Then they could come out and let people know that the pirates were home from the high seas.

When Huck and Joe understood Tom's plan, they laughed and cheered. Their fight was forgotten. All was forgiven. It would be all right to wait until Sunday. No other boy could say that he had gone to his own funeral and lived to tell about it!

Chapter ⑨

The Pirate Funeral

The boys made a solemn promise to go back to civilization on Sunday. Then they ate fish and bacon for dinner and went straight to sleep, completely exhausted by the day's events.

Joe woke up in the middle of the night. Something was wrong. It was very, very dark. Heavy rain clouds had covered the moon. The air felt hot and still. Flashes of lightning began to light up the sky, and thunder rumbled in from a distant place. A cool breeze chased away the hot air. The wind made a loud moaning noise in the trees.

Joe awakened his friends. A bad storm was coming up fast. Big drops of rain began to hit the ground. "Run for the tent!" Tom shouted, and they all took off. The boys huddled together under the old sail. Lightning flashed every minute now. It made a weird light in the pouring rain. Thunder boomed and crashed so loudly that the boys held their ears. It felt like the end of the world. The wind was bending

the trees and breaking off branches. The river sent big white waves crashing against the sand. This was no night for young boys to be outside!

The storm reached its worst point. The wind blew so hard, it ripped the old sail from about the boys' heads. Their tent went flying into the Mississippi. The boys ran for shelter under a giant oak tree at the river's edge.

Luckily, the storm moved on before daylight. As the sun came up, all was quiet once more. The boys had been badly frightened. They were also soaking wet. They went back to their campsite and saw that their sycamore tree had been struck down by lightning! It was a good thing they hadn't been under it when it fell.

The heavy rain had put out their fire, but Huck noticed a smoldering place on a big log they had used. There was a patch of glowing coals on the underside that had been protected from the rain. Joe and Tom looked underneath other logs in the woods for bark and small twigs that were still dry. Huck used them to start the fire again. Soon the big fire was hot enough to warm the boys and dry their clothes.

Saturday turned out to be beautiful and sunny. It was the boys' last day on the island. By this time, they were tired of being pirates, so they played at being Indians. They were all chiefs, of course. Using mud, they painted stripes on their faces and bodies and made war on one another all day.

The pirate Indians ate their last dinner on the island. Then they got ready to leave. It was sad to go, but it was also very exciting to sneak back into town. After dinner, Huck found a big log. He dragged it into the river, where it began to float. All three boys sat on the log and paddled across the river on it. When they landed on the Missouri shore, five or six miles downriver from St. Petersburg, they walked until they came to the woods at the edge of town. It was dark and very late by this time, so the boys slept there until early morning.

Nobody was awake yet when Tom, Joe, and Huck walked quietly through town. They hid in the upper gallery of the church. There were some old benches up there, but nobody ever used the gallery anymore. The three runaways could sleep there until they heard the church bells. They would be able to see and hear everything that happened at their funeral. And nobody would see them until they were ready.

That Sunday, the church bells rang slowly and sadly to show that somebody had died. The whole town came to church that day. Everyone looked very serious, especially the children from school. Tom saw that Becky Thatcher was even crying a little.

Aunt Polly, Sid, Mary, and the Harpers were the last people to enter the church. They were all dressed in black. They sat in the front row, near the minister.

The minister made a great speech about the boys. "It is true," he said, "that Tom Sawyer and Joe Harper and Huckleberry Finn played a lot of tricks on people. It is true that they made us impatient and angry a lot of the time. But they were all good boys at heart. Wild, maybe, but smart and kind and noble, too."

The minister said a lot of other nice things. He was trying to make people feel better, but everyone was crying, anyway. Even the minister began to cry.

No one noticed the small noises coming from the gallery. The boys climbed down outside, then opened the door of the church. People turned around as they heard the door squeak open. Then they stood up and stared. The minister couldn't believe what he was seeing. The dead boys were walking up the center aisle of the church!

"It's a miracle," he shouted. "Let us sing our thanks unto the Lord!"

Chapter

10

Tom's Marvelous Dream

People in St. Petersburg were so glad that the boys were back safe and sound that no one had the heart to punish them for their mischief. Aunt Polly spent all of Sunday scolding and hugging Tom. She was so relieved that he was safe. But she would kill him if he ever ran off like that again!

Aunt Polly was still talking about Tom's pirate adventure Monday at breakfast. "It was a good trick, Thomas Sawyer, to make us suffer for nearly a whole week while you boys had a good time," she said. "But if you really cared about your poor old Aunt Polly, you would have found a way to tell me you were all right. I was worried sick about you."

"Tom would have told us if he had been able to," Mary said.

"Sid would have thought to tell us," Aunt Polly continued. "Sid wouldn't have worried me so. Sid cares more about me than some other boy I know."

"I do too care about you," Tom protested. "Why, I even dreamed about you on Wednesday night."

"Dreaming's not much—a cat does that much—but it's better than nothing. What did you dream?" Aunt Polly wondered.

"I dreamed you were sitting by your bed. Sid and Mary were sitting on the wood-box," Tom began.

"That's nothing special. We always sit that way."

"But this time, Mrs. Harper was over here with you."

"Well, I'll be. She certainly was here Wednesday night. Do you remember any more?" Aunt Polly believed in dreams and prophecies. She was superstitious.

"I remember lots of things," Tom boasted. "The door blew open, and you made Sid go shut it."

"Why, so I did!" Aunt Polly exclaimed. She was getting more and more excited.

"You and Mrs. Harper were talking about me and Joe. Mrs. Harper said she was sorry about spanking Joe for drinking the cream when she really had thrown it out herself. Then Sid said he wished I hadn't been such a bad boy. You got mad and told him not to say such things. You said that God himself would take care of Tom Sawyer." Tom was enjoying himself now.

"It happened just that way. An angel must have been there with us all! Wait until Sereny Harper hears from me about this. She'll never laugh at me again for believing in spirits."

Tom wanted to tell Aunt Polly the best part. "Then Mrs. Harper left, and Mary and Sid went to bed. You prayed for me. When you fell asleep, I left a message on your table. It said, 'We are not dead. We are only off being pirates.' At least, that's what I think it said."

"So you did think of me! What a sweet boy you are, Tom Sawyer, even if you do turn my hair gray with worry most of the time." Aunt Polly was so impressed by Tom's dream that she gave him a big apple she had been saving. Then she hugged him and sent him off to school with Sid and Mary.

Tom and Joe were the envy of every child at school. The younger children followed the suntanned pirates around

wherever they went. The older boys couldn't even talk to them, they were so jealous.

But the girls loved to hear the stories Joe and Tom told about Jackson's Island. These stories were so full of exaggeration that you might have called them tall tales or just big lies. Joe told Amy Lawrence that he had been under that sycamore tree when lightning struck it. And Amy believed him!

As a result of all this attention, the boys became terribly stuck-up. Tom had decided that he would live for glory. He told himself that he didn't care if Becky Thatcher never spoke to him again. Unfortunately, the very day he gave her up forever, he saw her looking at picture books with Alfred Temple at recess— Alfred Temple, that smarty-pants from St. Louis, with his fancy clothes and his new shoes.

Tom was so jealous, he saw red. How could Becky Thatcher be so cruel when

she knew how much he liked her? Well, he had fought with Alfred Temple the first day that boy came to town. And he might just decide to fight him again. Tom had clearly forgotten that he hadn't been very nice to Becky, either. Getting engaged to Becky and then telling her about Amy Lawrence! Now she was doing the same thing to Tom. It was only fair.

It was obvious that Becky was avoiding Tom. She was still mad at him. That was clear. Tom went home after school feeling pretty miserable in spite of his heroic day. When he got home, he soon found out that Aunt Polly was mad at him, too.

"Thomas Sawyer!" Aunt Polly cried as soon as she saw him. "How could you let me go over to Sereny Harper and tell her all that nonsense about that dream. She knew all about how you came over here Wednesday night. Joe told her. You made a fool out of me, Tom. I feel like a total fool."

Tom had thought that his dream story would make a good joke. Now he saw that he had hurt his aunt's feelings.

"What am I going to do with a selfish boy like you?" Aunt Polly was upset. "You never, ever think about how other people feel. You ran away and had fun, but you never thought about us. Then you tell me that lie, and I get laughed at for telling it to one of my best friends."

"I didn't mean to be selfish," Tom said. "I'm sorry, Aunt Polly. I was wrong to tell that lie about the dream. But I was going to leave you that message. I wrote it on some sycamore bark."

"Are you lying to me again, Tom Sawyer? I can't stand it if you are telling another one of your lies!"

"I promise you, it's true! I did have that message in my pocket. It said, 'We are not dead. We are only off being pirates.' I didn't want you to worry." Tom seemed ready to cry, so Aunt Polly gave in. She did believe him, in spite of herself.

That night, when Tom was asleep, Aunt Polly looked for that old jacket Tom had gone pirating in. Would she find the message in his pocket? Was Tom really telling the truth? Aunt Polly hesitated twice before reaching in the pocket. When she pulled out the sycamore scroll and read Tom's message, tears began running down her face.

"He did write to me, bless his heart," she whispered. "I could forgive him a thousand tricks for this sweet message."

Chapter
(11)

Muff Potter's Trial

After all the excitement over his disappearance, Tom's summer vacation seemed to start off slowly. There just wasn't that much to do. Some of the kids from school had parties. Each party was grand, but they ended so quickly. And you had to wait such a long time for the next one.

A circus came to St. Petersburg for a while. That was terrific. For three days after the circus left town, Tom and his friends made their own circus. They made a big tent out of old sheets, and people paid one penny to see the pirate clowns do their tricks.

The summer days kept getting longer and more boring. Tom tried to keep a diary, but nothing happened for three whole days, so he gave it up.

To make matters worse, it rained all day on the Fourth of July. Tom was bitterly disappointed. The parade got canceled, and no one could light fireworks.

Shortly after July 4, Tom got the measles. He had to stay in bed for two weeks. His throat hurt, and he had a bad

fever. He had itchy bumps all over his body. Tom wanted to scratch them, but Aunt Polly said she would spank him if he did, because he would make scars. Tom was absolutely miserable for those two weeks. He had to stay inside, and he couldn't see any of his friends. He was very lonely. He felt like a prisoner in his own bedroom.

When Tom finally felt better, Aunt Polly let him go outside again. Everyone in town was talking about Muff Potter's murder trial. The townspeople were certain that Muff was guilty. They were convinced that he was the worst villain St. Petersburg had ever known. He was bloodthirsty and evil and no good.

Tom felt sick again when he heard all the bad things people were saying about Muff. Muff hadn't killed Doc Robinson. He was innocent. He had never hurt anybody. And he had also been Tom's friend. Muff had fixed Tom's kites and his fishing poles when they were broken. He had given Huck food when Huck was hungry, even though Muff often didn't have enough to eat himself. How could Huck and Tom keep quiet about what they had seen at the graveyard?

Tom was sick with guilt. He began having bad dreams at night again. He went to the courthouse each day of Muff's trial, but he didn't have the courage to go in the courtroom and listen. Huck felt the same way.

After the second day of the trial, the boys went to visit Muff in jail. Huck brought the prisoner some tobacco and some matches. Tom brought him some candy and some apples he had been saving.

Muff was very happy to see the two boys. "No one comes to visit me," he said. "I'm glad my friends Tom and Huck haven't turned against me. I've done a lot for the boys of this town, but they've all forgotten me. I've mended their kites, and I've shown them the best spots for fishing. But do they come to see me? No. The only friendly faces I've seen lately are yours."

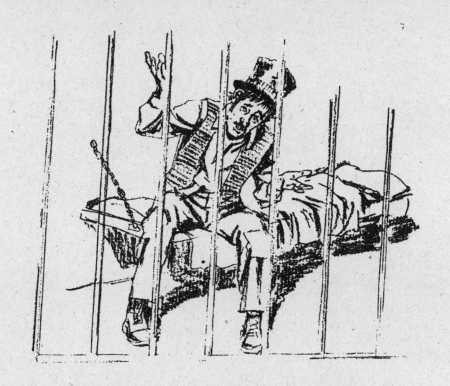

Muff thanked Tom and Huck many times for their gifts and for their visit. He shook their hands when it was time for them to leave. The boys couldn't possibly ever feel any worse than they did when they left the jailhouse.

"What are we going to do, Huck?" Tom wailed.

"I wish we had never gone to that graveyard," Huck moaned. "I wish we could just run off and hide somewhere."

"We can't let Muff Potter die!" Tom protested. "He'll hang if we don't tell what we saw, that's certain."

"Injun Joe is in that courtroom every day," Huck reminded Tom. "He just sits there, as calm as can be. But what will he do if we get up and tell? He'll kill us, that's what he'll do! And that's certain."

Huck was right. Injun Joe was a dangerous man. But the next day was the last day of the trial. Somebody had to do something, or Muff Potter would die for a crime he didn't commit!

Tom got home very late that night. He climbed in his bedroom window while Sid was sleeping. Tom had a hard time falling asleep, tossing and turning in his bed, he was so excited.

The next day, Tom had the courage to walk up the courthouse steps and enter the courtroom. He felt nervous, but at least he didn't feel guilty anymore. Tom sat down on a bench and looked around. The men and women of St. Petersburg

filled every single seat in the courtroom.
Injun Joe sat near the window. He looked
as cool as a cucumber sitting there. Huck
was there that day, too, but he and Tom
were careful not to look at each other in
front of Injun Joe.

The sheriff brought Muff Potter into
the courtroom. Muff had chains around

his hands and his feet. He looked pale and frightened and uncomfortable. Everyone was staring at him. Then the prosecutor and Muff's defense lawyer came in. The judge entered the courtroom last. When he sat down, the last day of Muff Potter's murder trial began.

The prosecution had to prove to the jury that Muff Potter had killed Doctor Robinson. The prosecutor began that day by reading Injun Joe's statement at the graveyard. Then he brought some witnesses to the stand.

The first witness had seen Muff Potter washing in the creek the morning after the murder. Muff had run away when he saw him watching. The second witness had found the knife in the graveyard. He had seen Muff Potter use that knife many times before. The knife that had killed Doc Robinson was definitely Muff Potter's.

Several more witnesses spoke to the judge and jury about how scared and guilty Muff Potter had looked when the sheriff brought him to the graveyard after the murder. Muff had cried out and almost fainted when he saw Doc Robinson's dead body.

When the prosecution had finished, it seemed that Muff Potter would hang for the murder of the doctor for sure. How could the jury decide that he was not guilty, after hearing all the testimony? The prosecutor had made a good case. His witnesses were some of the most honest people in St. Petersburg.

The strange thing was the reaction of Muff's defense lawyer. He didn't seem to be defending his client very well. Every time there had been a chance to cross-examine those witnesses, he refused. Did he believe that Muff was too guilty to defend? Was he just being lazy? What was that defense lawyer going to do now that he had to make his case for Muff Potter's innocence?

As the prosecution summed up its case against Muff, people in the courtroom began to whisper. Muff was certainly going to be convicted. And his own lawyer hadn't done much to defend him. It didn't seem like a fair trial. Muff groaned out loud. Huck squirmed in his seat, looking miserable. Injun Joe had a trace of a smile on his face.

Just then, Muff's lawyer said, "I would like to call Thomas Sawyer to the witness stand."

There was a murmur of surprise as Tom walked to the front of the room. He sat down and promised to tell the whole truth and nothing but the truth. Tom looked as white as a ghost, he was so scared. You could barely hear him speak as he answered the first question.

"Where were you on the night of May seventeenth around midnight?" the defense lawyer asked.

"In the graveyard, sir," Tom whispered.

"Were you anywhere near Hoss

Williams's grave?" pursued the defense. "Could you talk a little louder, please, when you answer the question?"

"I was hiding right by it," Tom said.

"Where were you hiding?"

"Behind the elm trees that grow there." Injun Joe's mouth twitched when he heard that.

"There was someone hiding with you, wasn't there?" Tom nodded yes. "That's all right," the lawyer said. "You don't have to say who was with you. We can save that information."

Huck sighed quietly with relief.

"Now, Tom, tell me," said the lawyer. "Did you take anything with you when you went to the graveyard?"

Tom looked confused.

"Your friend was carrying something. You can tell us. Don't be afraid."

"A dead cat, sir. We were carrying a dead cat because we wanted to take off some warts with it." There was a ripple of laughter in the courtroom.

"We will show the court the skeleton of that dead cat," Muff's lawyer declared. "Now Tom, I want you to tell us exactly what you saw that night in the graveyard. Just tell it like it happened. Take your time. Don't skip anything."

Tom told the whole story, but he was very careful not to mention Huck by name. There was silence in the courtroom when Tom got to the part about how Muff Potter had fallen and Injun Joe had grabbed the knife.

"What happened next, Tom?" the defense lawyer asked.

Shock went through the courtroom and everyone turned to look at the murderer. But before anybody could move, Injun Joe leaped off the bench and jumped out the window. He was loose, and now Tom's life was in danger!

Chapter

12

The Hunt
for Buried Treasure

Tom's picture appeared on the front page of the county paper the day after Muff Potter's trial. He was a hero whose courage had saved an innocent man from death. Unfortunately, the real killer had escaped in the most desperate manner. The paper announced the offer of a reward for the capture of Injun Joe. Professional detectives had been sent from St. Louis to look for clues, and the sheriff planned to knock on every door in the county. The authorities were confident that Injun Joe would be arrested and jailed in a matter of days.

Tom and Huck waited anxiously for news of Injun Joe's arrest. Until he was behind bars, they were both in danger, especially Tom.

It was fine to have your picture in the paper and to be the envy of every boy for miles. It was great to have your Aunt Polly fuss over you and tell you a hundred times a day how proud you've made her. It was okay to be a hero in the daytime, when there were adults all around you to protect you. But it was different at night. No one could convince Tom to set foot outside after dark.

Tom started having bad dreams again. Injun Joe would surely come back and get the boy who had ratted on him. And he would find out who that friend of Tom's was who'd been in the graveyard and kill him, too!

Many, many days passed with no sign of Injun Joe. Then, Tom began to relax. No news was good news. Maybe Injun Joe had run so far away, he was gone for good. Tom began to think about other things, like buried treasure.

There comes a time in every child's life when the desire to hunt for buried treasure is too strong to ignore. That moment had come for Tom, and now he just needed someone to help him dig for it. Joe Harper was out of town. Ben Rogers had gone fishing. That left Huck, the Red-handed. Huck always had time for a new adventure.

Tom found Huck at their favorite swimming hole.

"Where will we dig?" Huck wanted to know.

"Almost anywhere," Tom replied.

"Why? Is it hid all around, just anywhere?"

"Oh, no," Tom explained. "It's hidden in special places—sometimes on islands, sometimes in rotten old chests under the limb of a dead tree, where the shadow falls

at midnight. But mostly, treasure's hidden under the floor in haunted houses."

"Who hides it?"

"Robbers and pirates, of course. Who do you think?"

"Why do they hide it? If it were mine, I wouldn't hide it. I'd spend it and have a good time."

"So would I, but robbers don't. They always hide it."

"But don't they come and get it after a while?" Huck was a very logical young man.

"They think they will, but they generally forget the marks, or else they die. Anyway, the treasure lays there a long time and gets rusty. Sooner or later, somebody finds an old yellow paper that tells how to find the marks," Tom explained patiently.

"Have you got one of those yellow papers, Tom?"

"No."

"Then how are we going to find the marks?"

"I don't need any marks to dig. I told you already. They always hide it in a haunted house, or on an island, or under a dead tree that's got one limb sticking out. We've already looked on Jackson's Island. Then there's that haunted house near the Still-House Creek. And there's lots of dead trees on Cardiff Hill, behind the Widow Douglas's house. Loads of dead trees."

"Is it under all of them?"

"Of course not. Are you crazy?"

"Then how are we going to know which one to pick?"

"We'll look under all of them."

"You're the crazy one, Tom Sawyer. It'll take all summer to do that!"

"So what? Suppose we find a brass pot with a hundred dollars in it, or a rotten chest full of diamonds?"

Huck's eyes glowed. "You can keep the diamonds. A hundred dollars is enough for me!"

Huck was more than ready to start digging. The boys grabbed some tools— an old shovel and a crippled pick—and set out for a particularly promising dead tree in the woods on Cardiff Hill. They worked until they were all hot and sweaty. Then they sat down to rest a bit.

"I like this," said Tom.

"So do I."

"Say, Huck, if we find a treasure here, what are you going to do with your share?"

"I'll have a piece of pie and a glass of soda every day, and I'll go to every circus that comes along. That'll be swell!"

"I'm going to buy a new drum, and a genuine sword and a red necktie, and a bulldog puppy. And I'm going to get married," Tom declared.

"Married!"

"That's right."

"You *are* crazy! That's the worst thing you could do! You'll be fighting all the time, just like my mom and dad."

"The girl I'm planning to marry won't fight."

"Oh, but they're all alike. You just better think about it before you do anything you'll be sorry for." Huck thought a minute, then he got curious. "What's her name, anyway?"

"I'll tell you sometime—but not right now. We've got to keep digging."

Huck and Tom worked and sweated for half an hour. No results. They dug another half hour. Still no results. Huck

leaned on his shovel. "Do they always bury it as deep as this?" he wondered.

"Sometimes, not always," Tom said, sighing. "Not generally. I guess we haven't got the right place."

So Tom chose a new spot and they began again. Digging was terribly hard work. Both of the boys were getting tired. "Where are we going to dig next, after we finish this one?" Huck asked.

"I think we should try that old tree right behind the widow's house. You know the one I'm talking about."

"That'll be a good one," Huck agreed. "But won't the widow take it away from us, Tom? It's on her land."

"Just let her try. Whoever finds one of these buried treasures, it belongs to them. It doesn't make any difference whose land it's on."

Huck was satisfied with that answer. They started fresh on the tree Tom had just named. They both began to dig with renewed enthusiasm. Unfortunately, luck was against them that day, and they didn't find a thing. Finally, Huck had had enough. "Darn it, we must be digging in the wrong place again. What do you think?"

"I don't understand what's going wrong," Tom admitted. "Sometimes witches interfere."

"That can't be it. Witches don't have power over you in the daytime."

"That's true." Tom thought a minute. Suddenly it occurred to him. "I know what the matter is! What fools we are! You've got to find out where the shadow of the limb falls at midnight! Then you dig."

A whole day's work wasted! But at least Tom had figured it out now. They agreed to meet at Tom's that night. Huck arrived and meowed under Tom's window around ten o'clock. They walked to the tree and waited for what felt like forever. Being out in the woods at night wasn't much fun anymore. Thoughts of

buried treasure weren't quite enough to chase away thoughts of Injun Joe, who might be hiding somewhere nearby.

When Huck and Tom agreed it must be midnight, Tom marked the spot where the shadow fell, and both boys began to dig as fast as they could. The hole got deeper and deeper. Tom's hopes rose every time Huck's shovel hit something hard. But it was usually just a rock or a tree root. Tom eventually called a halt to it. "It's no use, Huck. We're wrong again."

"We can't be wrong. We marked that shadow to the dot!"

"But we only guessed at the time. It was probably too early or too late."

"That must be it. I don't want to dig under trees anymore, anyway. We'll never get the time right, and I don't like being here so late. I feel like someone's watching me. I've been creeping all over since we got here."

"Me, too," Tom said. "You know, they almost always put in a dead man's body when they bury treasure under a tree. To look out for it."

"Lordy!" Huck gasped.

"Yes, they do! I've always heard that."

"I don't like to fool around much where there's dead people, Tom. We're still in trouble for the last time we did that."

"I don't like to stir them up, either. Suppose this one here was to stick his skull out and say something."

"Stop it, Tom. Don't say such things! I'm more than ready to dig somewhere else."

"How about the haunted house near Still-House Creek?" Tom suggested.

"That's worse than digging at night. There's ghosts in haunted houses."

"We'll go in the daytime. Ghosts don't come around and bother you when it's light outside."

Huck thought it over carefully. "Well, all right," he said. "We'll tackle the haunted house if you want to. But it's taking a chance, I reckon."

Chapter

⑬

The Haunted House

Tom and Huck met at the haunted house the next day. They stood outside with their digging tools for some time before they had the courage to go inside. It was a large frame two-story house sitting all by itself near Still-House Creek. It had no fences or gate, and the grass in the yard had grown so tall, it reached the porch.

The house had been empty for as long as the boys could remember. All the windows were knocked out, and there were holes in the roof. The chimney lay in ruins, and the front door had come off. When the boys ventured to walk inside, they saw peeling paint and huge cobwebs everywhere. The floorboards downstairs had all rotted away, so the boys were standing on a carpet of grass in what used to be the living room.

Tom and Huck had never been in a haunted house before. The search for treasure was momentarily forgotten in their excitement over exploring. The boys put their tools in a corner of the living room and took a tour of the ground floor.

The staircase leading upstairs looked tempting, although the wooden steps looked pretty rotten and unstable. The boys dared each other to try it out and see what was upstairs. They were both a little nervous, though, about cutting off all possible retreat. If anybody were to catch them in that house, there would be no way to escape from the second story—the windows were too high to jump from safely.

The second floor turned out to be a disappointment. Even the closets were

empty. Tom and Huck were about to head back downstairs when they thought they heard something.

"What's that?" Tom asked in a terrified whisper.

"Sounds like voices coming through the yard."

"Get down on the floor and don't move a muscle," Tom warned.

There was a knothole in the wood of the floor near the place where Huck was lying. He inched over until he could see everything that was going on in the living room. "It's that deaf-and-dumb Spaniard who's been in town lately," Huck whispered. The Spaniard had a friend with him, a rough-looking man Huck had never seen before.

"I thought we'd never make it back here," the stranger said. His companion, the Spaniard, sat down heavily near the

ruined fireplace. "Yeah, it's been tough going with me ever since that cursed Tom Sawyer ratted on me at that trial." That was no deaf-and-dumb Spaniard! That voice belonged to Injun Joe. What a disguise!

Injun Joe pulled a bag from the pile of rubble that was once the fireplace. The boys upstairs could hear the jingle of coins as he counted them.

"Hey, Joe, don't you think we got enough there to leave for Texas like we planned?"

"One more job and then we'll go. We're going to clean out the Widow Douglas's house, and we're going to do it soon, tonight or tomorrow night. She's the richest woman in town. And that's not all. I've got half a mind to kill her for what her husband did to me," Injun Joe snarled.

"Okay, Joe, take it easy. We'll get her, and then we'll beat it to Texas. But what are we going to do with the loot we've got now? Leave it here?"

Injun Joe took out a handful of coins. "Yeah, you're right. Six hundred and fifty in silver is too much to carry. We'll take fifty and leave the rest." Injun Joe took out his Bowie knife and began to dig near the pile of stones where he was sitting. He had barely started when he hit something solid.

"What in the. . . ," Joe grunted as he began to clear away dirt with his hands. "Looks like a box. A metal box."

"I think I saw a shovel in the weeds over there." Joe's partner brought over the shovel and pick the boys had left in the corner. Tom and Huck cursed themselves for their carelessness.

Injun Joe and his friend made quick work of digging up that iron box and prying it open. Hundreds of gold coins glittered in the soft light of early evening. Injun Joe laughed when he saw all that money. "And I always thought those stories about the Murrel gang treasure were just a bunch of lies," he boasted.

"There must be thousands of dollars here. Why don't we just take this and forget about the Widow Douglas?"

"We're not going to forget about it because I want my revenge, do you hear?" Injun Joe snarled.

"Well, all right, then. What are we going to do with all this? Should we bury it here like we were going to?"

"Yeah, I guess," Injun Joe said slowly. Upstairs, joy flamed up in the hearts of the two boys. Here was more treasure than they had ever imagined, and they would know exactly where to dig!

Joe picked up the shovel, muttering

to himself. "Wait a minute," he said. "This shovel had fresh dirt on it when you handed it to me. Somebody has been here. In fact, they might be here now. They might just be upstairs!"

Tom and Huck looked at each other in utter panic. No place to run, no place to hide, no time to do anything, because Injun Joe was coming up the stairs!

Fortunately for the boys, Injun Joe was a heavy man, and the steps were in bad shape. He got about halfway up when the whole staircase just collapsed underneath him.

"That'll teach you to be so suspicious," Joe's friend teased as he helped him to his feet.

"It's not funny," Injun Joe growled. "Anyway, they might just come back at any time. They could see fresh dirt around this fireplace and know something was up. We're taking everything with us. We'll put the money in my den."

"Which one?"

"Number two—under the cross. The other place is bad—too many people around."

The two men packed up and left once it was completely dark outside, carrying the chest with them. What bitter luck for Tom and Huck! The treasure hunters were sorely disappointed once they had stopped feeling so frightened. Neither of them had the slightest idea as to where Injun Joe's den might be, but they committed his words to memory in the hope of further clues. They also agreed to keep watch over the Widow Douglas's place. If those robbers came near, they would run and tell the Welshman Mr. Jones, who lived just down the hill. He and his grown sons would be able to handle that old Spaniard and his friend! Tom agreed to watch that night, and Huck the next. Then the two friends went their separate ways. Tom had a picnic to go to the next day.

Chapter

(14)

McDougal's Cave

Becky Thatcher had finally coaxed her mother into organizing a picnic. Invitations had been sent to all of Becky's friends and schoolmates. The ferryboat had been hired to take the party three miles downriver to McDougal's cave.

Saturday morning, dozens of children came trooping down to the ferry landing carrying picnic baskets full of delicious things to eat and drink. They were ablaze with excitement at the thought of playing games all day and exploring the cave.

Parents didn't usually participate in picnics. It was enough to send chaperones—several young men and women who could watch over the younger children while having fun themselves. Since the party would last all day, some parents made arrangements for their children to spend Saturday night with friends who lived close to the ferry landing. Mrs. Thatcher told Becky that she should ask to spend the night with Suzy Harper and then go to church with the Harpers the next day. Tom told Aunt Polly he would stay with Ben Rogers or some other friend that night.

Neither Mrs. Thatcher nor Aunt Polly would have guessed that Becky would forget all about asking Suzy as soon as she saw Tom at the picnic. It wasn't until church was over on Sunday that anyone realized that the two children were missing and that something was terribly wrong.

Church service had just ended

when Mrs. Thatcher caught sight of Mrs. Harper, who was listening to Aunt Polly tell her all about the failed attempt to rob the Widow Douglas's house the night before. "Some boy told Mr. Jones that robbers were planning to stake out the Douglas place last night," Mrs. Harper was saying. "Mr. Jones took his three boys along and, sure enough, they spotted those rascals just where they had been told to look. It's a shame they didn't catch those villains, though."

"I wonder who that boy was who told

Mr. Jones? It wasn't your Tom, was it, Polly?" Mrs. Harper said, laughing.

"I doubt it. Mr. Jones said the boy made him swear not to reveal who he was to another living soul. My Tom would have been boasting all over town by now," Aunt Polly said, chuckling.

"Speaking of Tom, where is my Becky this morning?" Mrs. Thatcher asked Mrs. Harper. "She must have had such a grand time yesterday, you let her sleep late this morning."

Mrs. Harper looked puzzled.

"She did stay with you last night, didn't she?" Mrs. Thatcher asked.

"Why, no."

Mrs. Thatcher turned pale and sank down into a pew. Mrs. Harper and Aunt Polly began to look around anxiously.

"Joe Harper, have you seen my Tom this morning?"

"No, ma'am."

"When did you see him last?"

Joe tried to remember, but he wasn't

sure he could say. People had stopped moving out of the church. A murmur of uneasiness swept through the congregation as children and young people were questioned. No one had noticed whether Tom and Becky were on the ferryboat when it left McDougal's cave Saturday night. One young man finally blurted out his fear that they were still in the cave!

Within five minutes the church bells were frantically calling the whole town to

assemble for this emergency. Half an hour later, two hundred men were pouring out of town, heading for McDougal's cave to search for the missing children.

McDougal's cave was a limestone cave in the bluffs three miles downriver from town. Halfway up a steep hill overlooking the Mississippi, an oak door shaped like the letter "A" blocked the entrance to the cave. Behind the door lay the first chamber, sixty feet high. Beyond that, a tunnel about six feet wide led down about three-quarters of a mile to the main attractions of the cave—The Drawing Room, The Cathedral, Aladdin's Palace. Smaller tunnels branched everywhere off the main tunnel, creating a maze of crooked corridors, a perfect place for playing hide-and-seek. You could hide from other people in your group for up to half an hour without being found and without going beyond the known portion of the cave.

McDougal's cave was dangerous

precisely because no one knew all of it. It was just too enormous, extending for miles underground into the bluffs. If Tom and Becky had gone beyond the known portion of the cave and gotten lost, there wasn't much chance of ever finding them.

Monday morning, Judge Thatcher sent word from the search party at the cave: "Nothing yet. Send more candles and food."

By Tuesday, Mrs. Thatcher had fallen ill with fever. Searchers had found one of Becky's hair ribbons below the words "Tom and Becky," written in the candle smoke in a section far from the known portion of the cave. Mrs. Thatcher clutched that ribbon as the last relic she would ever have of her little girl.

By Wednesday, four days and nights had passed since Tom and Becky had entered the cave. Not many of the men searching for them had the hope or the strength to keep looking. Most of them gave up and went home, but Judge Thatcher and a few others kept trying, leading themselves with ropes far down into passages no one had ever set foot in before.

Bells tolled wildly again on Wednesday night, this time calling joyously to the searchers in the cave and to

all the mournful souls in St. Petersburg. Tom and Becky had been escorted home in a wagon, from a town eight miles downriver.

Tom and Becky were still very weak from their ordeal, but they managed to tell what had happened. "We played hide-and-seek with the others for a while, but we got to talking, and then we just drifted and talked, looking at things," Tom explained.

"There was this really neat waterfall made out of rock crystal. It made an arch, so I went behind it with the candle so that Becky could see the crystals, and I found this stairway. We made a big smoke mark so we'd find our way back. Then we walked down the stairs until we got to this huge room with pillars made of stalagmites and stalactites joined together."

"That's how we got lost," Becky chimed in. "There were thousands of bats hanging from the ceiling—thousands and thousands of them," Becky shuddered. "They didn't like the light

from our candles and they began to fly down. We ran down every passage we could find, but they kept chasing us. One of them put out my candle, but luckily, Tom had his or we wouldn't have been able to see at all."

"We knew we were lost when we got to this underground room we had never seen before," Tom continued. "We tried to find our way back, but it was no use. We made smoke marks to show where we had been, but there were just too many passages, and every one looked alike."

"We walked for hours and hours but we had no idea what time it was or whether it was day or night," Becky explained. "I got so tired and so hungry, I couldn't walk anymore. We had only a piece of cake that we had saved from lunch, and Tom gave me most of his share, but I just couldn't keep going." Becky started to cry again, and so did Mrs. Thatcher.

"We finally just had to stop where we knew we'd have water, at least," Tom said. "We listened until we heard water dripping and went to where there was a little stream running down the rock. We were so tired, we slept for a long time. I didn't want to tell Becky, but we were down to our last piece of candle."

"That was the worst part," Becky whispered. "We watched that candle melt until there was nothing left. Then it went out and it got so dark, you couldn't see anything, not even your hand right in front of your face! I just cried and cried, then, because I knew we were going to die in that cave. Tom tried to get me to move, but I was so tired and hungry, I just wanted to give up."

"I knew then I had to do something to get us out of there, so I told Becky I would go exploring, but I promised her I'd keep coming back to check on her. I had some kite string in my pocket that I tied around a rock near Becky. I tried two passages, crawling on my hands and knees because I couldn't see, making sure I kept hold of the string. Both passages ended in a sort of jumping-off point. I couldn't feel the ground under my hands and I didn't know if the drop down would be two feet or two hundred feet, so I had to come back."

"But the third passage worked!" Becky exclaimed. "When Tom came back and told me he had found a way out, I didn't believe him, but he begged and pleaded with me until I had to go see! I have never, ever been so happy to see a little speck of blue sky."

"We wouldn't have seen it at all if it had been nighttime outside," Tom added. "We squeezed ourselves through that hole and just sat down and cried and cried, we were so happy to be out of that cave!"

"We were on a hill looking down at the river. Those men who brought us home were on the river when they saw us. They couldn't believe we had come from McDougal's cave. 'You're five miles downriver from the entrance!' one of them said."

At this point it was clear that all of the excitement had been too much for two young people who had just survived four days and nights in a cave with little food and water. Tom and Becky were examined by a doctor and ordered to stay in bed and rest for at least a week. Aunt Polly and the Thatchers saw to it that the doctor's orders were strictly followed.

Chapter

(15)

Treasure at Last!

When Tom was finally allowed to leave his bed, a week later, the first person he wanted to see was Huck Finn. He found his friend lying on a flatboat moored at the river's edge.

Huck had been ill, too. He was the boy who had told Mr. Jones about the robbers, of course, but he had spent so long outside in the chilly night air and he had been so scared that he had fallen ill with fever. The Widow Douglas had taken care of him while he was sick.

"I didn't want him to, but Mr. Jones told the widow I was the one who saved her from Injun Joe and that other man," Huck explained. "Now I think she's making plans to adopt me. I heard her saying to Mrs. Rogers how it was a shame that my momma died and my dad had gone off and left me, probably, since no one's seen him for so long."

Huck sighed. "Don't get me wrong, Tom," Huck said. "I like the Widow Douglas, and she's been awfully kind to me, kinder than anybody's ever been to me before. But I just don't know about getting adopted. She doesn't like it when I curse, and I'll have to go to church and wear shoes and use a knife and fork when I eat. This September I know she's going to want to send me to school. . . ." Huck rattled off some other complaints.

Tom needed some time to think about Huck's situation before he could give him any advice. For the moment, he had another adventure to propose. "Huck, I think I know where Injun Joe's treasure is buried. I didn't tell anyone, but when

Becky and I were in McDougal's cave, I saw Injun Joe himself."

"You didn't!" Huck gasped. "Did he come after you?"

"I think he was just as scared to see me as I was to see him. I screamed, and he took off running."

"He probably thought you were a ghost or something," Huck mused.

"Maybe, but here's the good part. Right where he was standing, there was

this cross made with candle smoke on the ceiling. That must be den number two—'under the cross.' And I know exactly where it is. All we have to do is go back to the cave and get the treasure!"

"No one can get into McDougal's cave anymore!" Huck wailed. Tom looked puzzled. "Don't you know? The day after you and Becky got out, Judge Thatcher had a big iron door welded over the entrance to the cave. And he's got the keys."

Tom turned pale. "That was over a week ago, Huck," he whispered. "Injun Joe is still inside, and he can't get out!"

The two boys ran to tell Judge Thatcher, who went with the sheriff and his deputies to unlock the door. Injun Joe's dead body lay stretched out on the other side, his Bowie knife broken in two pieces nearby. He must have known it was hopeless, but he had hacked away at that door with his knife until the knife broke, to give himself something to do, something else to think about. He had

died of hunger and thirst. A broken sta-
lagmite had left a little hollowed-out
place in the stone, a kind of cup where
dripping water collected—one drop every
twenty minutes, one teaspoon every
twenty-four hours.

Injun Joe was buried at the mouth
of McDougal's cave. To this day, Injun
Joe's Cup stands first in the list of mar-
vels people come from miles around to
stare and shudder at.

Tom and Huck were sorry that Injun
Joe had died that way, but they were also
relieved that he wasn't going to come
after them anymore. They were free to
roam the woods and roads of St.
Petersburg again.

Hunting for that treasure was still
high on Tom's list. "We don't have to go
through the main entrance of the cave,"
Tom explained to Huck. "We can go in the
way I came out. I've marked the spot. We
can row down there today, if you're feeling up to it." Huck was still a little weak

from his recent bout with fever. But when Tom promised to do all the rowing, he agreed to go.

The boys gathered some shovels, candles, matches, and lunch, then borrowed a boat. When they got to Tom's spot, he said, "This bluff looks the same for miles and miles. But do you see that white place up there where there's been a landslide? That's one of my marks."

They unloaded the boat and walked up the hill. "Now, Huck," Tom continued, "where we're standing right now, you could touch with a fishing pole that hole I got out of. See if you can find it." Huck searched, but he didn't see anything. Tom marched proudly into a clump of bushes and pushed some aside. "Look at it, Huck," he said triumphantly. "It's the best place in the county for a robbers' hideout. You keep quiet about it, only we'll let Joe Harper and Ben Rogers in because it's got to be a whole gang or there won't be any style to it. *Tom*

Sawyer's Gang—sounds splendid, doesn't it, Huck?"

Huck agreed, and the two boys entered their new hideout to look for treasure. Tom led the way to the cross. A big rock stood underneath it, and four passages branched out from the room they were in. The boys tried the passages first, but found nothing. They came back and rested against the big rock.

"Could it be buried here, under this rock?" Tom wondered. He got out his

Barlow knife and began digging. Four inches under the surface, he struck wood. The boys used their shovels to dig up what turned out to be long wooden boards covering the entrance to a natural passage underneath the big rock. They followed the passage down to another cavern directly underneath the room they had just been in. Inside it were guns and blankets and the treasure box!

Tom and Huck were beside themselves with excitement. Now they had a real robbers' hideout and a box so full of gold coins, it must have weighed fifty pounds! Luckily, Tom had thought to bring canvas bags to put the money in. They filled the bags and staggered down to the boat with their loot. Tom rowed back upriver to St. Petersburg and then borrowed Benny Taylor's red wagon to put the bags in.

The treasure hunters neared the Widow Douglas's woodshed, where they were going to count and divide everything. But just before they got there, Mr. Jones caught up with them. "We've been looking all over for you two," he said happily. "Come along with me—everybody's waiting for you at the widow's place. You boys trot on ahead, I'll pull the wagon for you. Why, it's heavy. You hauling bricks or old metal?"

"Old metal," Tom said carefully.

"I thought so. The boys in this town

spend more time looking for junk than they do working jobs, and they end up making half the money." Tom and Huck grinned at each other.

When they all arrived at the widow's, Aunt Polly took one look at the boys' muddy clothes and hustled them upstairs. She supervised clean-up and dressing personally. They had to wear new suits, ones the widow had recently bought for Huck but which were uncomfortable enough to make both boys equally miserable.

Aunt Polly led her gentlemen back downstairs to the dining room, where guests were assembled for what looked like a big party. An important event. Huck looked torn between the desire to run away and the desire to stay and eat all the good things on the table. Tom shot him many sympathetic glances.

Sure enough, this was Huck's official adoption party. The Widow Douglas was celebrating her decision to take Huck in and raise him right. She would spend the money necessary to educate him and set him up in some small businesses.

Tom couldn't keep silent any longer. "Huck's not poor! He's got money! He's rich!" There was an embarrassed silence at the table. Everyone knew that Huckleberry Finn had never had as many as two nickels to rub together, poor thing.

"You don't believe me, but I'll prove it to you!" Tom insisted. He ran outside and came staggering in under the weight of the bags. He poured the mass of gold coins on the table. "There! What did I tell you! Half of it's Huck's, and half of it's mine."

It was more money than anyone present had ever seen before. After another moment of stunned silence, an explanation was demanded, and provided by Tom. For weeks afterwards, Tom's theories about buried treasure were repeated all over town. Every empty house in St. Petersburg was taken down, board by board, and its foundations dug up and sifted for hidden treasure. And not by boys, either, but by men—pretty serious, unromantic men, too, some of them.

Chapter

(16)

The Education of Huck Finn

Tom's money was put in the bank at six percent interest. Huck's, too. And Huck did get adopted by the Widow Douglas, since he really couldn't manage all that money by himself. Life had almost settled back down to normal when Huck turned up missing.

People looked for him for two full days. The Widow Douglas was frantic, because she really cared about her adopted son. Luckily, Tom knew where to look for him. The second night, he slipped away from the search party and found Huck himself, in an empty shed behind the old slaughterhouse.

"I'm not going back, Tom," Huck warned as soon as he saw his friend. "I'm sorry. I like the widow a lot, but I just can't stand living that way. I suffocate in those suits she makes me wear—I can't sit down or roll around or get any air. She won't let me smoke and I can't curse and I have to ask permission to go everywhere, even swimming! You can have my share of the money, Tom, just give me a dime now and then. Not more than a dime. I don't seem to care about a thing that's not hard to come by."

"You know I can't let you abandon the widow, Huck. It's not fair. Besides, you might come to like it at her house if you stick with it a little longer."

"I'd like it about as much as I'd like a hot stove if I sat on it long enough!" Huck declared. "No, Tom, I won't be rich, and I won't live in those stuffy houses. I like the woods and the river. And I'll stick to them. And just when we were going to be robbers! We had a hideout and everything. It's all spoiled!"

Tom saw his opportunity. "Being rich isn't going to keep me from starting a robber gang at our hideout, Huck. But I can't let you in the gang if you're not respectable, you know."

"But you let me be a pirate," Huck protested.

"That was different. A robber is more high-toned. In most countries, they're awfully high up in the nobility—dukes and kings and such. And all robbers have been to school."

"You wouldn't shut me out of the gang, would you, Tom? We've always been friends," Huck said pleadingly.

"I wouldn't want to and I don't want to, but what would people say? Why, they'd say, 'Mph! *Tom Sawyer's Gang,* pretty low characters in it.' You wouldn't like that, and I wouldn't, either."

Huck was silent for some time, engaged in a mental struggle. Finally, he said, "Okay. I'll try it at the widow's again for a month and see if I like it.

You'll let me belong to the robber gang then, right, Tom?"

"It's a deal, Huck. And I'll ask the widow to let up on you a little."

"Will you really, Tom? That'd be grand. If she'll let up on the roughest things, I'll try not to curse and I'll wear those stupid clothes and I guess I'll go to school. When are we going to start the gang and turn robber?"

"We'll have the initiation tonight."

"What does 'initiation' mean?"

"It's where you swear not to tell the gang's secrets, even if you get chopped to pieces for not telling. And you've got to have the initiation at midnight, in the scariest place you can find—a haunted house is best."

"They're all ripped up now."

'That's true. We'll go to the graveyard, then. You've got to swear on a coffin and sign with blood!"

"Wow! It's a million times better than pirating. I'll stick with the widow if it kills

me. When I'm the best robber ever, and the whole county's talking about it, she'll sure be proud she took me in out of the cold," Huck concluded.

And that was how Tom Sawyer's friend Huckleberry Finn acquired some manners and a good education.

THE END

ABOUT THE AUTHOR

Samuel Langhorne Clemens was born in 1835 in Florida, Missouri. He left home in 1853 and tried several different careers.

In 1863, Clemens first used the pseudonym "Mark Twain" as his signature on a humorous letter. Little did he know then how famous that name would make him.

He published his first novel-length book in 1869, followed by many others. The events recorded in *The Adventures of Tom Sawyer*, published in 1876, are said to be an accurate account of the author's own adventurous childhood antics.

Samuel Clemens died in 1910, along with Mark Twain, leaving great gifts for the world and a name that will live on forever.

Treasury of Illustrated Classics

Adventures of Huckleberry Finn
The Adventures of Pinocchio
The Adventures of Robin Hood
The Adventures of Sherlock Holmes
The Adventures of Tom Sawyer
Alice in Wonderland
Anne of Green Gables
Beauty and the Beast
Black Beauty
The Call of the Wild
Frankenstein
Great Expectations
Gulliver's Travels
Heidi
Jane Eyre
Journey to the Center of the Earth
The Jungle Book
King Arthur and the Knights of the Round Table
The Legend of Sleepy Hollow & Rip Van Winkle
A Little Princess
Little Women
Moby Dick
Oliver Twist
Peter Pan
The Prince and the Pauper
Pygmalion
Rebecca of Sunnybrook Farm
Robinson Crusoe
The Secret Garden
Swiss Family Robinson
The Time Machine
Treasure Island
20,000 Leagues Under the Sea
White Fang
The Wind in the Willows
The Wizard of Oz